Omar On Ice

Maryann Kovalski

Fitzhenry & Whiteside • *Toronto*

For Thomas Kovalski

Text and Illustrations copyright © 1999 Maryann Kovalski

Published in Canada by Fitzhenry & Whiteside, 195 Allstate Parkway, Markham, Ontario L3R 4T8

Published in the United States by Fitzhenry & Whiteside, 121 Harvard Avenue, Suite 2, Allston, Massachusetts 02134

www.fitzhenry.ca   godwit@fitzhenry.ca.

10 9 8 7 6 5 4 3 2 1

National Library of Canada Cataloguing in Publication

Kovalski, Maryann
Omar on ice / Maryann Kovalski.

ISBN 1-55041-507-7 (bound).--ISBN 1-55041-783-5 (pbk.)
I. Title.

PS8571.O96O42 1999a   jC813'.54   C99-931300-2
PZ7

U.S. Publisher Cataloging-in-Publication Data
(Library of Congress Standards)

Kovalski, Maryann.
Omar On Ice / Maryann Kovalski.
2nd edition.
[32] p. : col. ill. ;   cm.
Summary: Omar aspires to be a famous artist; however, when his teacher misinterprets his drawing of his mother for a rock, Omar loses confidence and throws his artwork in the trash.
With the support of his friends, he tries to take another look at his art.
ISNB 1-55041-507-7
ISBN 1-55041-783-5 (pbk.)
1. Friendships -- Fiction. 2. Self-confidence -- Fiction. 3. Artists -- Fiction. I. Title.
[E] 21   1999   AC CIP

First published in hardcover in 1999 by Fitzhenry & Whiteside.
First paperback edition, 2002

Fitzhenry & Whiteside acknowledges with thanks the Canada Council for the Arts, the Government of Canada through the Book Publishing Industry Development Program (BPIDP), and the Ontario Arts Council for their support for our publishing program.

Cover and Book Design by Wycliffe Smith Design

Printed in Hong Kong

Omar On Ice

Omar loved pictures.

When he grew up, he was going
to be an artist. People would come
from all over to have him paint their
portraits. Maybe they would pay him
with candy. Omar liked red ju-jubes best.

Omar could not wait for school tomorrow.
Maybe Ms. Fudge would hold up
his picture in front of the class.

When Ms. Fudge passed out the paper and pencils,
Omar felt the paper's smooth surface.
He loved the bright yellow of the pencil.

"I'm going to draw my rock collection," said Thomas.
"I'm making a rocket," said Bart.

"I will make a daisy," said Elsie.
Elsie drew every kind of flower.
She made it look so easy.

Soon the whole class was quietly
working away. Only Omar sat staring at his paper.

"What's wrong, Omar?"
asked Ms. Fudge.
"I can't think of anything
to draw," he said.
"Why don't you try
drawing something you love?"
suggested Ms. Fudge.

This gave Omar an idea.
He picked up his pencil
and started to draw.

"Ms. Fudge is going to
love this," he thought.

"What lovely rocks,
  Thomas,"
said Ms. Fudge.
  "Thank you," said Thomas.

When Ms. Fudge saw
Omar's drawing,
she was delighted.

"Why, Omar, this
picture is wonderful!"
Omar beamed.

"Look, class," said Ms. Fudge. "Hasn't Omar drawn a beautiful rock?"

"That's not a rock," said Omar. "That's my mother." Ms. Fudge looked again. She turned the drawing this way and that. "Yes, I see her now. Lovely." But Omar was not happy.

Ms. Fudge moved down the row and held up everyone's pictures, one by one.

"I'm a bad artist," growled Omar.

"Maybe it's your paper," said Elsie.

"Maybe you need another kind of pencil," said Thomas.

"It's not my pencil. It's me," said Omar.

Omar threw his drawing away.
"I'm just a bad artist," he said.

The bell rang for recess.

The whole class hurried outside.

Everyone laced up their skates and got on the ice—
even Ms. Fudge. Everyone, except Omar.

"Why aren't you skating, Omar?" asked Thomas.
"You're the best skater in the whole class."
"I don't care if I'm the best skater. I want
to be the best artist," said Omar.

17

Elsie skated by. She did not
skate as well as
she drew flowers.
She fell down hard
on the ice. Omar
went to help her up.

"Rats," she said,
  "I can't skate."
   "Maybe your skates are
   too big," said Omar.
    "It's not my skates.
    It's me. I'm just a bad skater."

"You're trying too hard," said Omar. "The thing about skating is to have fun. It's easy when you don't worry. Watch."

Omar took off slowly,
gliding like a bird in the sky.

Then he skated backwards like a sailboat
against the wind.

When he picked up speed,
he zoomed like a fast car.

Omar skated this way and that.
He whirled and swirled
from one end of the pond
to the other.

Soon Omar forgot all about being a bad artist.
He was having too much fun being a great skater.

When he jumped high in the air,
the whole class cheered.

"Look at Omar," said Thomas.
"Look at the ice," said Elsie.

On the ice were beautiful lines
wherever Omar had skated.

Elsie saw a turtle.
Thomas saw a bird.
Ms. Fudge was sure she saw Omar's
mother smiling.

It was true. Omar had drawn
many beautiful pictures on the ice.
Even he could see how good his drawings were.

"I was right," said Thomas,
as they made their way home.
"You just needed a different
kind of pencil."